RORY
and his
Magic Castle

STORIES ®

Author: Andrew Wolffe   Illu... ...n Cole

Text and illustrations copyright © K... ...003.
The Rory Stories is a Registered Tra... ...blishing.
First published 2000. This edition pub... ... . 0 9534949 2 6

A CIP catalogue record for this book is a... ...the British Library.

Printed in Singapore

KEPPEL

Keppel Publishing Ltd.
The Grey House, Kenbridge Road,
New Galloway, DG7 3RP, Scotland.

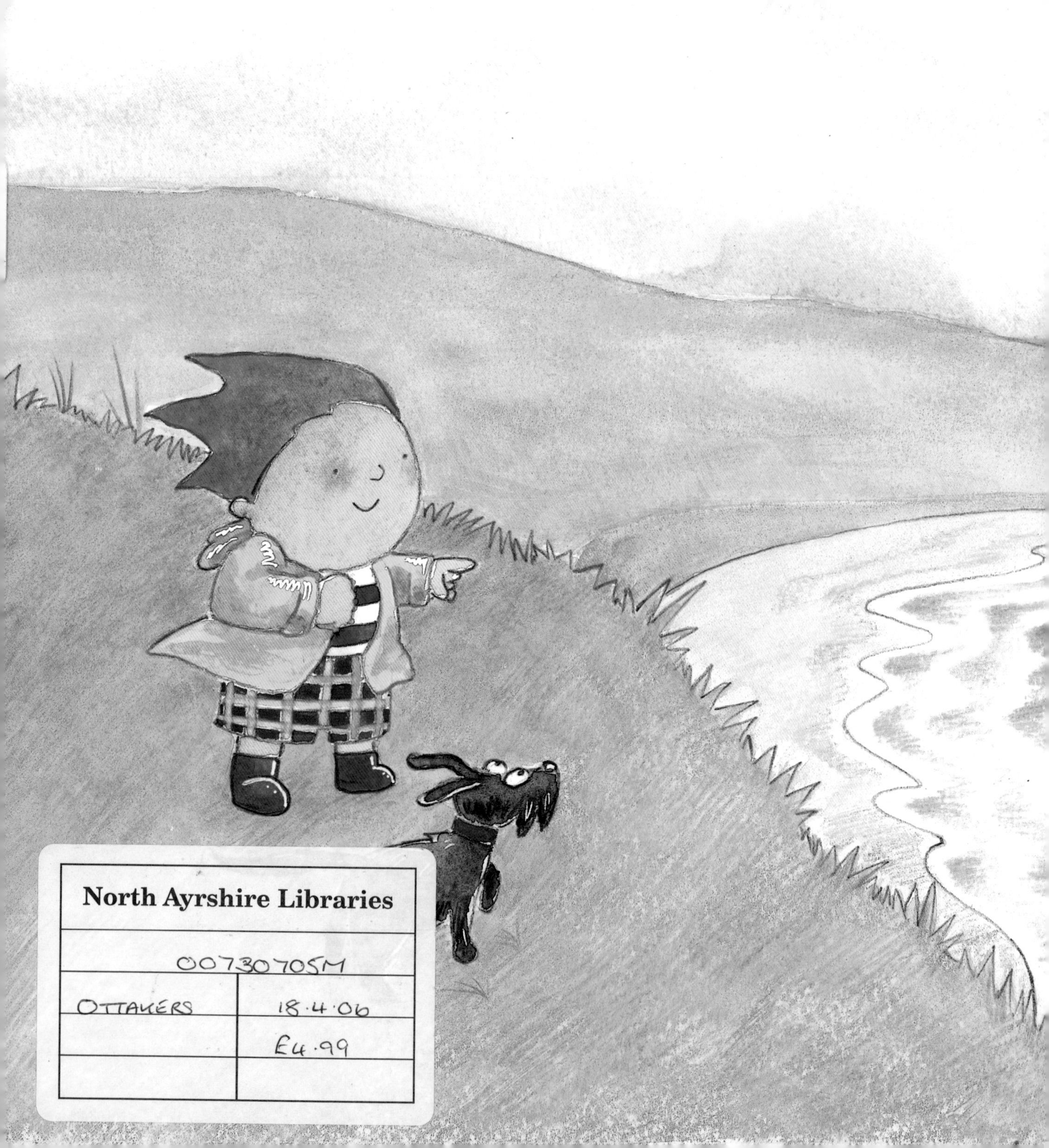

It's never very hard to find Rory and Scruff McDuff. On most days they usually play on the beach that stretches for ever and ever in their village by the sea. Even stormy weather and wild winds don't stop them from visiting their most favourite place in all the world.

Rory had decided to build a sandcastle with his new bucket and spade. Not just any sandcastle: it was going to be the biggest ever seen in Sandy Bay. Rory started by filling bucket after bucket with sand.

Scruff McDuff, who as always was keen to help, used his paws to dig. Sometimes he was a little too enthusiastic and sprayed sand all over himself and Rory.

"Take your time Scruff McDuff," laughed Rory as he shook the sand from his raincoat and emptied his wellingtons.

Rory and Scruff McDuff worked busily for what seemed like ages. But despite all their efforts, they had only managed to build the foundations of the sandcastle.

"Whew," exclaimed Rory. "At this rate we'll never get it finished before the tide comes in. What we need is an extra pair of hands."

"Perhaps I can help?" came a deep voice from behind a nearby rock pool.

Startled by the unexpected visitor, Rory turned to face a huge octopus.

"**I**'m a stranger to these shores," explained the octopus with a friendly smile. "I was washed up on the beach on the crest of a big wave last night. To tell you the truth, I'm a little bored waiting around until the tide gets high enough for me to swim off. I would be glad to lend a hand, so to speak."

"I can do the work of four people, thanks to these," the octopus continued as he waved his extremely long tentacles in the air.

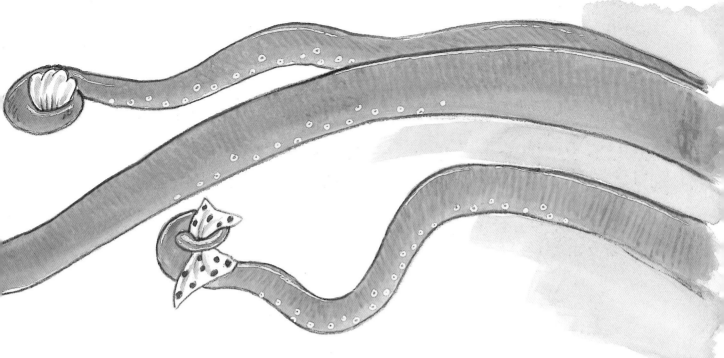

"And I can squeeze into all kinds of places," he added, cheekily dropping some tentacles into Rory's pocket and pulling out, one after the other, a seashell, a handkerchief and a banana with several loud SUCKS!

Despite Scruff McDuff's obvious disapproval, Rory could see that the octopus would be a great help to them and agreed to let him join in the fun. Rory explained his plans to make the sandcastle really special and the octopus came up with a few suggestions of his own.

With Rory, Scruff McDuff and the octopus working together it didn't take long before the sandcastle started to grow...

...and grow...

...and grow, until
its turrets and ramparts
towered high above
them all.

Rory fetched water from the rock pool to fill the moat and once the finishing touches had been added, they all stood back to admire their handywork. Just as Rory had planned, they had built a sandcastle that was the biggest ever seen in Sandy Bay.

ut there were also a few surprises
in store.

Much to Rory's delight, the sandcastle
was big enough to walk right inside. Then,
as soon as Rory and Scruff McDuff had
walked through the archway and entered
the courtyard, they had an unexpected
encounter.

"Allow me to introduce ourselves - Lord and Lady Lobster and our little nippers," said Lord Lobster. "Welcome to Lobster Castle. Would you like a guided tour?"

"We'd love one," replied Rory, while Scruff McDuff tried to shake off one of the little nippers who had latched on to his tail. "But it's getting late and we'd better go home for our tea."

"You simply must return tomorrow when you have more time," suggested Lord Lobster, as he waved goodbye to Rory and Scruff McDuff at the door of his castle.

As Rory and Scruff McDuff walked home, the weather suddenly became more stormy. The wind howled through the sand dunes and huge waves rolled in from the sea and crashed on to the beach.

"I expect the octopus will be used to swimming in choppy water," Rory reassured himself and Scruff McDuff. "I just hope Lobster Castle will be alright."

The next morning all was calm again. Rory and Scruff McDuff went down to the beach to make sure the Lobsters were alright. But when they reached the spot where Lobster Castle had proudly stood, not a trace of it remained.

"It must have been washed away last night," said Rory sadly. "If only we had known that stormy weather was on the way, we could have warned Lord and Lady Lobster."

Feeling very miserable, Rory and Scruff McDuff were just about to turn back when a familiar voice suddenly rang out across the sand from the direction of the rock pool. "I say, over here. Delighted to see you old chaps."

Much to the relief of Rory and Scruff McDuff, it was none other than Lord and Lady Lobster and all their little nippers, safe and sound after all and looking no more than a little windswept.